AF604684

GIRLS SPORTS ACADEMY

Swimming

LAURA SIEVEKING

PENGUIN BOOKS

PENGUIN BOOKS

UK | USA | Canada | Ireland | Australia
India | New Zealand | South Africa | China

Penguin Random House Australia is part of the Penguin Random House group of companies whose addresses can be found at global.penguinrandomhouse.com.

First published by Random House Australia in 2017
This edition published by Penguin Books, an imprint of Penguin Random House Australia Pty Ltd, in 2024

Cover illustrations by Rebecca King © Penguin Random House Australia Pty Ltd
Cover design by Caroline Lee © Penguin Random House Australia Pty Ltd
Internal design and typesetting by Midland Typesetters, Australia

Printed and bound in Australia by Griffin Press, an accredited
ISO AS/NZS 14001 Environmental Management Systems printer

A catalogue record for this book is available from the National Library of Australia

ISBN 978 1 76162 032 4 (Paperback)

Penguin Random House Australia uses papers that are natural and recyclable products, made from wood grown in sustainable forests. The logging and manufacture processes are expected to conform to the environmental regulations of the country of origin.

penguin.com.au

We at Penguin Random House Australia acknowledge that Aboriginal and Torres Strait Islander peoples are the Traditional Custodians and the first storytellers of the lands on which we live and work. We honour Aboriginal and Torres Strait Islander peoples' continuous connection to Country, waters, skies and communities. We celebrate Aboriginal and Torres Strait Islander stories, traditions and living cultures; and we pay our respects to Elders past and present.

For my dad. Thank you for planting a love of words deep into my heart.

According to Greek mythology, Delphin was the god of the dolphins. He served the sea-god Poseidon and was sent on special missions for him. He was fast, sleek and beautiful. He was a creature of the water – the sea was his domain. His shining body would glide through the misty depths of the ocean, seeking out whatever Poseidon had sent him to find.

It was a story that ran through my head often. My mum had told it to me over and over as I went to sleep at night. You see, my name is Delphine and, like my namesake Delphin, I too am a creature of the water.

It was obvious from a young age that I was special when it came to the water. I was able to swim by the time I was two years old and by five I was swimming laps with kids twice my age. I was discovered by a coach from a renowned local swim school and he put me in their elite development squad when I was eight. I was training five mornings a week in every season of the year. But it was never a chore. Before the sun had even kissed the horizon, I would be awake in the darkness of my room, packing my swimming bag, ready for training. My poor parents were dragged out of bed at five o'clock in the morning to take me to my squads. But I think it was all worth it for them, as they huddled on the sideline with a rug and a steaming thermos of coffee, to see the glee on my face as I finished another lap. I'd wave to them on the viewing platform, giving them a big thumbs up. They would wave back and smile.

As time went on, juggling school and swimming training became difficult. Training became earlier and earlier in the morning so we could fit in enough sessions alongside school. I loved school, but every afternoon my eyes would be fixated on the classroom clock, willing the little hands to move faster towards home time so I could hit the pool or the beach.

If I wasn't at training, I'd be at the beach with my dad and my three older siblings. My dad is a keen surfer – he once represented Australia in surfing – and all my siblings have been water babies. My two brothers surf competitively and my older sister plays water polo for the state. We live right by the beach and we only feel complete if we have sand between our toes and crunchy sea-salt hair.

I remember my dad driving me to early-morning training one day when I was in Year 5. He said that he and Mum were exhausted by my training schedule as well as looking after the other three kids who had their own gruelling timetables. My heart was in my throat – where was he going with this conversation? In my mind that day, I decided that if he was going to make me quit swimming, I would run away to the ocean and become a mermaid and live in an underwater kingdom for the rest of my days.

Luckily, Dad wasn't asking me to quit swimming at all, which was fortunate as I wasn't exactly sure how to find this underwater kingdom. Instead, he told me about a school in the city that was the best sporting academy for girls in the country – a school where you did your schoolwork but also had time every single day to devote to your chosen sport. Girls from this school went on to the Olympics and other sporting halls of fame. It was called the Academy of Sport for Girls and it sounded like a dream come true.

The Academy was about a forty-minute bus ride from our house. It was also a boarding school, but I wouldn't need to stay there as I lived close enough to just ride the bus each day. This was a huge relief for me, as a life lived far from the beach seemed like no life at all.

Getting into the Academy was tough. I spent the rest of that year training the hardest I'd ever trained in my life. Every other swimming meet seemed irrelevant – the only thing I wanted was to get into this school.

Finally, after swimming meets, interviews and some academic testing, the results were in. They came in the form of a crisp, white envelope with the Academy logo on the top left-hand corner. I remember gazing at the school crest with its four quadrants. I ran my fingers over the images inside the crest – a lion, an eagle, a plume of feathers and the laurel leaves. Underneath were some Latin words which I couldn't read. I clearly remember my dad opening the letter for me – I couldn't look. I scanned his face eagerly, searching for a hint of disappointment or glee.

That was last year.

Which brings me up to this moment.

Here I was, shaking out my arms and legs as I approached the blocks. I glanced down at my Academy swimming costume and smiled. It was navy blue with a white trim and bore the Academy crest on the bottom left hip. I adjusted my swimming cap that had the Academy of Sport for Girls initials on the side. I felt someone squeeze my arm in encouragement. It was Melissa, another member of the 4 x 100-metre relay team. She was the first to swim as our strong backstroke swimmer. She offered me a nervous smile.

Next up would be Bec. Her specialty was breaststroke. She was shy by nature but a force to be reckoned with in the water.

Our butterfly swimmer was Ava. She is the tallest twelve-year-old I've ever seen and one of the best athletes I've met. She could have qualified at the Academy in athletics, basketball or netball, but swimming is her passion.

And then there was me. Delphine. Delphie-Dolphin, as the girls called me. I was the last to race as the fastest 100-metre freestyler at the Academy for our age group.

'Okay, girls, let's do this!' I yelled, jumping up and down. I'd become like the captain of the relay team – Coach Stuart had asked me to be in charge of psyching up the girls before the race. I know exactly why he chose me to do it – I was a ball of energy and positivity and nothing could shake my confidence. I'd always been the loudest person in any room and shyness was not a problem for me. Keeping my mouth shut sometimes was.

Melissa stood on the edge of the pool and took a deep breath. She plopped herself into the water and resurfaced, giving us a big smile. She held on to the side of the pool and adjusted her goggles.

'Time to win, girls, and time to kick some butt!' a voice yelled from the lane next to me. I looked over and saw Annabel Ogilvy clapping loudly to encourage her relay team. Annabel glanced at me with a cold, blank expression, then turned back to her team.

I knew Annabel because she was also the freestyle swimmer for their team. While I was the fastest freestyler at the Academy, she was the fastest freestyler at the National Swim School. They were our biggest rival. In most meets, it was either me or Annabel who took out the 100-metre freestyle gold. We'd swum against them in the qualifiers earlier and Annabel seemed to be swimming a little slower than usual. We qualified first and the National Swim School had come in second. I was quietly hoping maybe they were having an off day.

'Take your mark,' a crackly voice said over the speaker system.

Melissa crouched up against the wall, ready to push off.

BEEEP!

The backstroke swimmers launched themselves into the water and the race was in full swing. Melissa's long, lean body undulated through the clear water with her arms stretched out above her head. She'd made a good start.

Suddenly, the erratic splashing began as the backstroke swimmers surfaced. Melissa powered through the water at amazing speed with the Swim School backstroker just half a body behind. Melissa made a good turn and pushed out in front as she swam back towards us in her final lap. As her last arm stroke reached out for the wall, Bec was off.

The frenzied splashing of the backstrokers subsided as the heads of the breaststroke swimmers bobbed up and down in the water. The Swim School breaststroker was probably the best swimmer on their team. She quickly destroyed the lead that Melissa had created in the backstroke leg and overtook Bec at the tumble turn. But Bec wasn't giving up. She kept close to the Swim School swimmer, nipping at her toes the whole lap back.

I wasn't too nervous yet as I knew Ava would be our secret weapon in getting us ahead again on the butterfly leg. As Bec finished, Ava propelled her body into the water and began her thundering butterfly lap. Her wide, strong shoulders pulsed in and out of the water as she drove her body forwards. By the time Ava was heading back up towards our end of the pool, she'd regained the lead. She was a body length ahead of anybody else and I knew all I had to do was finish the job for a win.

I stood on the blocks, energy pumping through my body. It had been a huge day for me – qualifiers and finals in four races and this was my last race of the day. Even though I was exhausted, I knew I could do it.

I glanced to my side and saw Annabel Ogilvy yelling 'C'mon!' as she stood tall, ready to dive. It was going to be between the two of us. Annabel had swum just as much as I had that day, so she should have been equally tired. We were both running on empty tanks, but it was time to pull out any last drops of energy we had left.

As Ava thundered to the end of the pool, I launched myself into a long, graceful dive. The deafening roar of the water in my ears as I hit the pool signalled to my body that it was time to give everything I had. As I began into my freestyle stroke, I knew I had to finish this off for my team. The black line at the bottom of the pool raced by beneath me as I quickly reached the end of my first lap. I could feel Annabel just behind me – an eerie, threatening presence.

As the end of the pool approached, I felt my rhythm was a bit off. My tumble turn was too early and I didn't get maximum push-off for my second lap. I could feel Annabel tumble next to me and shoot out ahead.

I switched it up a gear and began to sprint.

But Annabel was like a rocket. Her swimming seemed far stronger than it had been in the qualifiers.

I knew I had to focus on my own stroke and stop worrying about what was happening in the next lane. I put my head down and channelled every ounce of strength I had left into finishing this race.

As I hurtled towards the finish, I gave it everything. I thumped my hand against the wall, ripped off my goggles and turned to the electronic scoreboard as the winners lit up one by one.

1. The National Swim School
2. The Academy of Sport for Girls
3. College of Sport
4. Hunterville Sports High

I didn't even read the rest of the placings. We hadn't won.

I looked up and saw the Swim School team pull Annabel Ogilvy out of the pool and hug her. They pumped their fists into the air and made a 'number one' sign with their fingers.

My team hoisted me out of the pool and gave me a pat on the back.

'Good swim, Delphie,' Ava said.

'I'm so sorry, guys, I let you down,' I said, shaking my head. I felt terrible.

'Second place is great,' Melissa smiled. 'We'll get them next time.'

As we moved to the side and grabbed our towels, I saw Annabel pull off her swim cap. Her long, dark hair tumbled down from her ponytail as she rubbed her face with her towel.

'You did it!' squealed a voice behind us.

Another girl, of identical height to Annabel – and with the same long, dark hair – ran up and hugged her. It was her identical twin sister, Ashley. Ashley was also one of the Swim School's better swimmers, although she wasn't quite as unbeatable as her sister, which was why she didn't swim in the relay. The Ogilvy sisters stood side by side, holding hands. They were towering girls, standing together in a seemingly unbreakable wall. One thing was for sure, if the Academy was going to take down the Swim School any time soon, we had to start beating the twins. Especially Annabel.

CHAPTER Two

We walked through the grounds in a line with our arms linked, the four of us taking up the entire path. We wore our Academy tracksuits with royal blue pants and a tracksuit top, zipped high up under our chins. That's just how swimmers wore them. Gymnasts seemed to prefer the baggy jumpers and equestrian girls wore their tracksuit tops zipped only halfway up with a turtleneck underneath. But the basketballers always walked around in their sleeveless T-shirts, even in the middle of winter. It was funny how you could tell what sport everyone was from just by looking at them.

On most days, we had to wear the very formal Academy uniform. In winter it was a crisp white shirt, a tie and a heavy, navy, striped tunic over the top. We also wore navy stockings and polished (yes, always polished!) black shoes. But today was Friday, a full training day, which meant we had sport for the entire day. We were allowed to go to school in our sports uniforms instead of changing halfway through.

'Delphie, what is your hair doing?' a voice asked from behind us.

Melissa, Bec, Ava and I unlinked our arms and turned to see Mrs Brunette, the school headmistress. I lifted my hand to my hair and realised I'd left it out again – long white-blonde hair flowing down my back.

'Oh, sorry, Mrs B!' I said hurriedly, as I bundled my hair into a ponytail.

'That's Mrs Brunette, thank you,' she replied, trying to hide a smile.

I pulled the elastic band from my wrist and wound it tightly around my hair.

'Ribbon or scrunchie?' Mrs Brunette added, with a raised eyebrow.

'Tada!' I yelled, pulling a ribbon from my pocket.

Mrs Brunette smiled, shaking her head lightly. 'Thank you, Delphie.'

As Mrs Brunette walked away, we linked arms again.

'You are hilarious, Delphie,' Melissa said.

'Why?'

'You talk to the principal as if she's your best mate! I'd never be brave enough to talk to her like that,' Melissa said. Melissa was a lot of fun but she was quieter by nature. She definitely wasn't a rule breaker, like I could be.

‘I’m not used to the hoity-toity at this school,’ I said, scrunching up my nose. ‘At my old school, there weren’t so many rules to remember! Ribbons, polished shoes, hair up at all times, regulation undies –’

Bec laughed. ‘Delphie! There are no regulation undies!’

‘There may as well be because everything else is regulation!’ I giggled. ‘And there was no “Miss” and “Sir” at my old school either – we called our teachers by their first names, and after school we’d end up down the beach surfing with them!’

‘Can you imagine Mrs Brunette on a surfboard?’ Ava cackled.

Mornings at the Academy always started with assembly. The grand Assembly Hall was located right at the top of the campus. We walked slowly along the path, passing the tennis courts and netball courts. As we snaked up through the school, we passed three lush green ovals with soccer and hockey goals set up, as well as the athletics track. The school was huge, and I'd learnt over my six months there that you had to give yourself a good ten minutes to walk through the grounds in order to get anywhere on time.

We stopped off at the building next to the Assembly Hall where all the Year 7 lockers and bag racks were. Girls were bustling about, sorting their belongings for the day.

'Hey, Delphie!' A blonde girl waved as she approached us.

'Oh, hey, Evie. Ready for the Science test tomorrow?' I asked.

'No!' She laughed.

I laughed too as she walked off. Evie was a lot like me – loud and always saying exactly what was on her mind. She was an Academy gymnast, although not the tiny type. She was tall for a gymnast and she looked strong and powerful. She was in my Science class and we'd become good friends when we were both moved to the front desk in the class for talking too much at the back.

Suddenly, the bell pierced through the air and the sound of lockers opening and slamming became more frenzied.

We walked across the quad, breathing in the crisp winter air. It was days like these that I was glad the school pool was well heated.

We approached the Assembly Hall and filed in with the mass of students. The hall was an impressive building – it was a huge auditorium with lines of bench seats in front of a giant stage.

'Squeeze in,' a teacher said as she ushered us to one of the rows. The four of us slid along the row towards the end and sat down. The room was buzzing with chatter and laughter until a single bell sounded and everyone ceased talking, immediately standing up.

Down the centre of the hall, a procession of the principal, the school captain and some of the teachers walked to the stage and tiptoed up the steps. All of them sat on seats which lined the front of the stage while Mrs Brunette stepped up to the lectern. She gently adjusted the microphone to her height.

'Good morning, everyone.'

'Good morning, Mrs Bruuuuuuneeeeettte,' everyone chorused.

'We shall begin with our school song,' Mrs Brunette said, as a soundtrack clicked on through the loud speaker.

Fields of green; pools of blue
Strength of spirit; hearts be true
Respect and courage; eyes on the prize
Through crushing lows and soaring highs
This is our school, where we learn and we strive
Strength in our bodies; spirits alive!
The Academy fire burning bright in our hearts
Focus in training; all taking part
This is our school, where we learn and we strive;
Strength in our bodies; spirits alive!

If there's one thing I'd learnt at the Academy so far, it was this: girls who are awesome at sport are not necessarily awesome at singing! But all the students sang with heart and gusto, including the teachers. As the track ended, we shuffled back down into their seats and awaited Mrs Brunette's next announcement. It was so quiet you could hear a bubble pop.

'Thank you, girls, nicely done.' Mrs Brunette smiled. 'Now, our school captain, Elise Goldburn, will give the morning announcements.'

Elise stood at the podium. She was a swimmer like us, which made us proud. She was in her final year of school and also swimming qualifiers for the National junior team. She was pretty amazing.

'Good morning, everyone. Congratulations to our senior gymnastics squad, who competed on the weekend in the state trials. Our senior team placed second overall and all eight gymnasts will move on to the second state trials. We wish them well.'

We all applauded.

'A reminder to Year 9 students – you will not have sports training for two weeks as you sit your half-yearly exams. Good luck!' Elise smiled. 'Swimmers – Coach Stuart has asked me to remind you to bring in your permission forms for your training camp next week. A note has been emailed home to your parents or to your boarding housemistress, if you are a boarder. It has a list of everything you need to bring on camp.'

I turned to my friends and smiled. We were really excited about training camp. The camp was for students of four elite swim schools from around the country. There were about twenty of us going from the Academy. It was a great opportunity to spend more time racing against the Swim School girls and learning about their strengths and weaknesses. And the best bit was, there was going to be a big swimming carnival at the end – the perfect opportunity for the medley team to win back our title against the Swim School.

Assembly finished with the national anthem and we bundled out of the hall in a stampede of chatter. Everyone raced back to their lockers to get their sports bags and the equipment they would need for training. I slung my swimming bag over my shoulder and joined my friends for the long walk down to the pool.

The aquatic centre was at the south end of the school, just before the boarding houses, the stables and cross-country land where the equestrian girls could ride their horses. This part of the school was beautiful – you felt like you were in the countryside, not the middle of a city. We approached the entrance to the main foyer and walked through the big glass doors, making our way straight to the change rooms.

Ava, Bec, Melissa and I pulled on our swimsuits. For training sessions we could wear what we wanted, I always trained in old and comfortable swimmers. For competitions, we wore special RASG racing skins – we all felt like Olympic swimmers when we put them on. I bundled my long, thick blonde hair up into a bun and stretched my swimming cap over my head with a snap.

'Let's go!' I said impatiently as Melissa struggled with her cap.

'Calm down, Delphie, we're not even late!' Bec laughed. 'You're such a keen bean!' Bec was always a voice of reason. She quickly pulled on her swim cap and grabbed her goggles.

'Okay, ready,' Ava said, slinging her towel over her broad shoulders.

The four of us walked in single file as we exited the change room and headed back through the foyer to the pool area. Or should I say, 'pools'. There wasn't just one pool at the Academy, but three. There was the long, fifty-metre competition and lap pool. It had eight lanes and starting blocks at the end. Above it was a huge flashing scoreboard and stop clock. On the other side of the pool was a deep diving pool. It had three heights of diving boards, including a ten-metre-high diving platform. I shuddered as I peered up at it. I was a pretty daring chick, but there was no way you would ever catch me jumping headfirst off that thing. Divers must be insane.

'Delphie! Mel! Bec! Ava!' a bright, deep voice called from the side of the pool. It was Coach Stuart. He was a tall guy with dark hair and massive, broad shoulders. He'd been a national rep swimmer in his day and had even qualified for the Commonwealth Games. Sadly, a shoulder injury hit him hard and he never fulfilled his Olympic dream. He always told us that he never regretted a day of his swimming career, even if he didn't meet that final goal. I wasn't so sure though. There was a sadness in his eyes that betrayed his jolly character.

'Oooh, are we doing underwater cameras today?' asked Bec.

'Sure are!' Coach Stuart laughed. He pressed a couple of buttons on his laptop, which was set up on a table at the side of the pool. Coach Stuart always laughed at how much training had changed since he was in the pool. In his day, it was all about swimming with a few aides and training tools, but now methods were really high-tech. The Academy had underwater cameras – little ones no bigger than a mobile phone – that linked up to a laptop by the side of the pool. The cameras filmed us from lots of different angles so we were able to scrutinise our starting dives, stroke technique and tumble turns. It was super fun.

As the final few girls filed out of the change room, Coach Stuart gestured for us to sit down on the pool deck.

'Now, before we begin training today, I have some info to give you about swim camp next week. As you know, camp runs for five days. Everyone must be here on time on Monday or else you will miss the bus. We will NOT wait for you. Second, I have met with the coaches from the other clubs coming on the training camp. We are excited to get you girls training with other people – it will be a really good experience. Remember, a lot of these girls will end up being on your team if you go to state or national titles one day. So be nice!' Coach Stuart said with one eyebrow raised.

We giggled slightly.

'No, I'm serious. I don't want any silliness with the other teams – particularly our biggest rivals at the National Swim School. I know some of you want revenge after the last meet, but this is not the time, got it?'

'Yes, Coach,' we all chorused.

'Good. Now, enough of that. Everyone get up and let's start training!' he boomed.

'Did you hear that, Delphie? Be *nice* to Annabel Ogilvy.' Bec giggled.

'I'm always nice!' I said, pretending to be offended. 'I'll just be kicking their butts too!' I smiled to myself. Sure, I was happy to 'get along' with everyone at camp … just as long as I could smash them at the same time!

CHAPTER Three

'Bye, Delphie, have an awesome time. And be good!' Dad said in a warning tone.

'What do you mean? I'm always good!' I laughed as I slung my sleeping bag over my shoulder.

'You know exactly what I mean, young lady. No mischief. And *think* before you act!'

I winked at him as I slammed the car door and waved. 'Bye, Dad!'

I dropped my bag to the ground as Dad

drove away, and pulled my jumper on over my head. It was a cold, clear morning and Dad had offered to drive me to school since we had to be there at seven o'clock ready for the camp bus. Butterflies fluttered about in my stomach in excitement.

I walked up the path towards the front gate, where a long bus was parked. Its undercarriage storage door was open and bags were piled in mounds around the wheels. A portly driver wiped his reddened face with the back of his hand as he carelessly hauled the bags into the bowels of the bus, one by one.

'Delphie!'

I turned and saw Melissa running towards me, arms outstretched. I gave her a quick hug and walked over to the rest of the gang.

'We are seriously going to freeze on this camp,' Ava wailed. 'My brother went there for rugby training a few weeks ago and he said the cabins were unbearably cold!' For such a tall, strong-looking girl, Ava could be a real softie sometimes.

Ava's brother was a rugby player at the boy version of the Academy. It was called the Academy of Sport for Boys and was our 'brother school'.

'I'm sure you'll be fine, princess,' Bec teased.

We bundled ourselves onto the bus and raced for the back seat. The four of us stretched out along the long bench at the back window. The cool kids at the back. Yes, I'll admit it, the four relay girls were the cool kids.

The journey began with the usual bus antics – trying to get passing trucks to blast their horns, playing spot the beetle-car, hair braiding and singing 100 renditions of 'The Ants Go Marching'. But after an hour or so the bus quietened. Some people fell asleep and others put on their headphones to listen to their own music. I gazed out the window in boredom at the passing cows – we were deep into farmland now.

I startled as another big bus drove up beside us. On board, there was a group of girls, waving and taunting through the windows. Up the back of the bus, right in line with me, were two matching faces with long, dark hair. They both glared at me. One raised an eyebrow in a light smirk. The Ogilvy twins.

I took in a sharp breath as their bus overtook us, much to the delight of all the Swim School girls. They waved out the back windows with their fingers raised in a 'number one' sign, as if their bus was beating ours in a race to the camp site. So much for 'nice'.

We followed the National Swim School's bus into a driveway with a sign marked 'Camp Birubi'. This was no ordinary school camp site. It was a training facility used by some of the top sporting teams in the country. It had topnotch facilities, including an Olympic-sized pool. Even some of the National Olympic teams had come to this site for team bonding and training sessions.

We trundled off the bus, stretching out our cramped limbs, and gathered in an outdoor undercover area. Slowly, the other swim schools arrived and more nervous girls sat down quietly. There was an air of awkwardness as we sat side by side with those we usually swam against. Some offered friendly smiles and others avoided eye contact altogether.

'Welcome!' a voice boomed from up the front. It was Coach Stuart. He stood before us, flanked by the coaching staff from the other swim schools. It was a pretty impressive line-up of coaches. A lot of them had swum in National teams themselves and others had coached girls who had gone on to Olympic glory.

I smiled in nervous excitement.

'This week is going to be fun but also hard work for you girls,' said Coach Stuart. 'We'll be starting training at 6.30 am each morning.'

There were a lot of muffled groans from the crowd.

'This means breakfast is at 5.30 am. Yes, you heard me, 5.30 sharp! The coaching staff are going to be pretty strict about you girls getting proper rest. We want you to eat properly – no skipping breakfast – and getting to bed on time. We will have lights out at eight o'clock.'

There were gasps from the girls. *Eight o'clock? That's a kiddy bedtime!*

The National Swim School coach, Vanessa Hartwell, stepped forwards. 'This means there will be NO shenanigans in the night. No getting up. No midnight feasts. No sneaking around. If we catch anyone out of their cabins after lights out, you will be banned from the final carnival on day five.'

'Speaking of the final carnival,' Coach Stuart added, 'I want you all to train hard so we can have some really good races on the day. The winners will not only get bragging rights, but they will also receive one of these beautiful medals.'

The coaches stepped aside to reveal a large table with an array of gold, silver and bronze medals. Everyone knelt up, craning to see the sparkling medals attached to long, smooth ribbons.

'I want gold', I breathed.

'Now, logistics,' Coach Vanessa said, flipping open her clipboard. 'I'll leave the list of cabin numbers here on the front table. Come up and find your name and cabin number and take a printed map of the camp site. The cabins are located in the southern area of the camp site, not too far from the aquatic centre, which is right next to the dining hall. We'll also be using the gym labelled 'Gymnasium Four'. We'll have fitness training sessions as well as our group meetings in there. You'll see on the map that behind the southern cabins there is a lake. That area is out of bounds. Understand?'

'Yes, Coach Vanessa,' we chorused.

Another coach from one of the other swim clubs stepped forwards. 'I'm Coach Matt, for those of you who don't know me yet. I just wanted to add that if you are all very well behaved, we have a fun surprise planned for you on Wednesday night!'

An excited chatter rose among the girls. Whispers of *disco* or *night swimming* flittered about in the air.

'Okay, find your bags and get settled into your cabins!' Coach Stuart beamed. 'We'll meet in the dining hall for lunch in one hour. And then training begins!'

We jumped to our feet and crowded around the list of cabins. My eyes scanned down the page until my name jumped out at me.

<u>Cabin Two:</u>

Delphine Attkinson

Melissa Wong

Rebecca Tonelli

Ava Cooper

I turned to my friends and squealed. 'We're together!' But then my eyes scanned back up the list, where two names jumped off the page.

Cabin One:
Ashley Ogilvy
Annabel Ogilvy
Rachel Peterson
Amanda Leong

'Oh, great,' I moaned as I walked with my friends to get our bags. 'The Ogilvy twins are right next door!'

We made our way down to our cabin and opened the door. Inside, there were two sets of unmade bunk beds. The room had a clean, cream carpet and crisp white walls. Adjoining the room was a small bathroom with a shower, sink and toilet.

'Hey, this is actually really nice!' Melissa said in surprise.

'Yeah, nothing like the cabins we had at my old school's camp.' Ava said, scrunching up her nose. 'Man, they were gross. The mattresses were dusty and brown and there were boogers stuck to the wall.'

'Eeeeeew!' we all screamed in unison.

'Bags the top bunk!' Melissa yelled as she threw her sleeping bag onto one of the higher bunks. I put my bag on the bed below hers and Ava also put her bag on a lower bunk.

'There's no way I'm going top bunk.' Ava laughed. 'I'll smack my head on the roof every time I sit up since I'm so tall!'

Bec happily threw her bag on the bed above Ava's.

We all looked up when we heard giggling from someone passing our open door. It was the Ogilvy twins, walking along with linked arms. One of them glanced into our room. 'Isn't it funny how you are cabin number two?' she asked, smiling at us through the doorway. 'And we are cabin number ONE. It's just like the last swimming meet, isn't it?'

The other twin laughed loudly at her sister's joke. I frowned. Melissa mouthed silently 'be nice'.

'Looking forward to training with you guys,' I offered.

The twins glanced at each other. 'If you can keep up,' one of them retorted. The second twin laughed loudly again as they walked into their cabin and slammed the door.

'They are so arrogant!' Bec scoffed.

'Well, wouldn't you be if you were an Ogilvy?' Melissa laughed. 'I mean, their mum won Olympic gold for Australia and their dad swam in the gold medal relay team for the USA. They have some serious champion heritage going on there.'

'Who cares who their parents are?' Ava said, shaking her head. 'We'll beat them where it matters – in the pool. Nobody cares who your parents are at the end of the race, when you are standing on that first-place podium.'

We unpacked our gear and chatted in excitement about the days ahead. When we noticed it was almost time for lunch, we put our shoes back on and started for the door. Much to our surprise, one of the twins was in the doorway.

'Are you guys heading up to lunch?' she asked.

'Sorry, are you Ashley or Annabel?' Bec asked. The Ogilvy girls were identical and there was no way of telling them apart without their help.

The twin paused, as if thinking about it. Melissa and I exchanged confused glances.

'Annabel,' she said coolly. 'I've forgotten where they said the dining room is – do you mind if I walk with you?'

'Sure,' Melissa said, shrugging. 'Where's Ashley?'

'Oh, she's gone ahead, I think,' Annabel answered quickly.

We exited the cabin in single file with Annabel at the back. My friends walked ahead, forming a group, and Annabel joined them, making polite small talk.

As I walked behind them, I heard the door of the twins' cabin quietly close behind us.

Strange, if Ashley had gone ahead, who was that? Maybe it's one of their other cabin buddies.

I shrugged and jogged to catch up with my group. But a peculiar feeling in my chest told me that something fishy was going on.

CHAPTER Four

'Lights out in ten minutes,' Coach Vanessa said, peeping around our door. 'When you hear my whistle blow, it's time for bed.' She shut the door and we began to change into our pyjamas.

'How are we expected to go to sleep now? I'm wide awake!' Bec moaned.

'Tell me about it, I'm way too excited about training and the carnival. Sleep is the last thing on my mind,' Ava sighed. 'Olympic champions have trained here, how cool is that!'

'Do you reckon any of us will … you know … make it all the way? To the Olympics?' Melissa asked hopefully.

'Ava will!' I laughed. She was the strongest swimmer at the Academy and had Olympic gold written all over her.

'Man, I would love to,' Bec whispered. 'Imagine if competitive swimming was your whole job. It would be amazing.'

'We need to be able to beat those Ogilvy girls first,' Ava said.

'Don't you reckon it was weird how Annabel was being strangely nice to us on the way up to the dining hall?' I asked. 'She seemed – I dunno – like she was up to something.'

'Oh, Delphie, you're such a drama queen,' Ava said, throwing a pillow at my head.

A whistle pierced through the night air.

'That's Coach Vanessa,' Bec said. 'Lights out before we get busted!'

Ava jumped off her bed and flicked the light switch off. The room went dark except for a sliver of moonlight peeking through a crack in the curtains.

'Night, everyone!' Melissa sang.

We each rustled open our sleeping bags and slithered into them, pulling them up to our chins to keep warm. As I slid my legs further into the bag, I noticed something long and thin brush against my foot. I yanked my foot away.

'Switch the light on! There's something crawling in my sleeping bag!' I yelped.

Ava leapt up and flicked the switch back on. I unzipped my sleeping bag, and there in the bottom of the bag was something long, scaly and black. I shrieked at the top of my voice, leaping out of my bed and onto Ava's.

'It's a snake! It's a snake!' I screamed.

Ava screamed too and climbed up the ladder onto Bec's bed. Melissa jumped from the bed above me onto Bec's top bunk and I flew up the ladder behind them, screaming at the top of my voice.

The door burst open and Coach Vanessa entered the room. 'WHAT is going on?' she yelled over our shrieks of panic. She looked furious.

'SNAKE!' we all squealed, pointing to the black slithery shape on my open sleeping bag.

Coach Vanessa peered over at my abandoned bed, then, shaking her head as she picked up the snake by its tail. 'Is this some kind of a joke?' she asked, her eyes piercing into us. It was now clear that the snake in her hand was a toy. 'We said no shenanigans, girls. This isn't funny!'

'We didn't do it!' Melissa cried.

'One of you thought it would be funny to play a trick on the other – that much is obvious. But this isn't funny. We said no silliness after lights out.'

'Somebody else did this!' I blurted out. 'We didn't do it!'

'I don't want to hear it,' spat Coach Vanessa, cutting off my pleas. 'Back into bed. And set the alarm on the table for five o'clock. You girls are now on breakfast set-up duty.'

'Five?' Bec shrieked.

'Yes. And if I hear another sound out of this cabin, you will be in big trouble. Do you understand?'

'Yes, Coach Vanessa,' we said sheepishly, as we climbed off Bec's bunk and back into our own beds. Coach Vanessa flicked off the lights angrily and shut our door.

'Where on earth did that snake come from?' Bec whispered into the darkness. 'Do you reckon your brother or one of his mates put it there before camp?'

'No, my brother and his mates are annoying but they're not *that* annoying,' Ava said.

'I reckon I know who did this,' I huffed. 'It's those Ogilvy girls.'

'You can't prove that, Delphie,' Melissa whispered, unconvinced.

'I told you they were acting funny earlier today. I know it was them,' I mumbled. 'We need to keep a very close eye on them.'

As I rolled over to go to sleep, I swear I could hear giggling on the other side of the wall in the cabin next door.

I know it was them. Who else has it in for me like that? And why had Annabel been so nice at lunchtime? They were giggling in the cabin next door right after we got into trouble. I mean, they could have put the snake in my sleeping bag at any point.

Ouch!

I yanked my hand back, which had just smacked onto the plastic lane rope. I glided to the end of the pool and stood up in the shallow end, adjusting my goggles.

'Delphie, what are you *doing?*' Coach Stuart yelled. 'Focus!'

I shook my head in frustration. He was right, I wasn't focused at all. Well, not on swimming anyway. I'd been slow in our warm-up and now we were swimming the main set of our training. We were doing some long-distance, lower intensity training today (as opposed to sprints, which we did in session one), with loads of 400-metre sets. But my mind had been wandering. Even though swimming looks like it would be relaxing and thoughtless, there is actually heaps to concentrate on while training. And my training was suffering because I was obsessing over those Ogilvy girls. If it was their aim to get in my head, they sure were succeeding.

As I finished my set, I hoisted myself out of the pool, panting lightly. In the lane next to me, I could see the twins at the other end of the pool. One of them stopped at the shallow end to take a breather. She seemed to be struggling a bit. As one tailed the other, the twins finished their laps slowly, pulling their exhausted bodies out of the pool.

'We still have to work on your fitness and stamina in the pool, girls. It's your weak spot,' Coach Vanessa said as she tossed them each a drink bottle.

'I just get so tired,' one of the twins moaned. I guessed it was Annabel. She was definitely the more vocal of the two.

Ashley frowned self-consciously. She always seemed on edge as if she was about to get into massive trouble. Ashley looked up and saw me listening in. I quickly turned away and grabbed my water bottle.

I wandered over to my friends, who had just finished a set as well. 'Have you noticed the twins struggling in training?' I asked, as I pulled my arm across my body, holding the stretch.

'Oh, Delphie, you have got to get over the twins!' Ava sighed.

'Actually, now that you mention it, I have!' Melissa said with surprise. 'When you were doing sprints this morning, you practically lapped Annabel. She's fast on her first lap, but she gets tired quickly. You seriously kicked her butt, Delphie.'

I chewed my lower lip thoughtfully.

'Maybe that's why they are so fast in competitions – it's just a few quick races,' Bec offered.

'I don't know about you, but I find comps exhausting,' I argued. 'If they can't even last a training session in the morning, how on earth are they getting the energy to swim six or seven races at top speed in one day?'

'It is weird,' Ava agreed.

'Girls, come over here,' a voice boomed from across the pool. It was Coach Stuart standing by his laptop, which was glowing brightly on a wooden trestle table. We wandered over to him with the girls from the other swim schools and Coach Vanessa.

‘We’re going to do some work on tumble turns today. I’ve got my underwater camera hooked up to my computer here and I’m going to film your turns.’

Some of the girls from the other swim schools cooed, clearly impressed. Not all the swim schools used the technology the Academy was lucky enough to use in training sessions.

Coach Stuart held up a small camera attached to a metal pole. He gently lowered the camera into the water and smoothly walked beside the pool, dragging the pole along with him.

‘Delphie, jump in!’ he called to me.

I leapt to my feet, smiling. Okay, I admit it, I’m a total show-off and I love everyone watching me.

‘Girls, watch the laptop screen as Delphie swims,’ he told the group, as I slipped my goggles on over my head. The girls from the other swim schools gathered around the laptop excitedly. 'Delphie, freestyle then tumble turn,' Coach Stuart called out.

I prepared to dive into the pool. I shook out my arms and launched my body into a soaring dive. The water crashed in my ears as I broke its surface. I swam measured, even strokes as I approached the end of the pool. I reached my right arm forwards, then tucked my body into a tight somersault. I twisted through my midsection and then extended both my legs together in a powerful kick. I felt the end of the pool on the soles of my feet as I pushed off the wall. I came to the surface and heaved myself out of the pool. I joined the other girls around the monitor as Coach Stuart tapped away at the buttons, replaying the footage of my tumble turn.

'See here, Delphie? You are turning just a bit early and not getting maximum extension of your legs when you kick off the wall. See?'

The footage showed me turning underwater. He was right – my legs were already partially extended before I kicked off the wall. I nodded.

'That's so cool!' one of the girls from another swim school exclaimed.

'Okay, Swim School girls, we'll work on filming yours next. Everyone else can warm-up their tumble turns in the other lanes, or come and watch the Swim School girls' turns on the laptop,' Coach Stuart said.

As the Swim School girls practised their tumble turns, I couldn't help but watch.

'Okay, Annabel, go!' Coach Vanessa instructed.

The girl laughed. 'I'm Ashley!'

'Oh, sorry – Ashley, you changed your goggles!'

Ashley swam to the wall and launched into a tumble turn. It was obvious on the monitor that she was turning too late. Her tumble was too close to the wall. She got out of the pool and watched herself on the monitor as Coach Vanessa pointed out the problems with her turn.

'See here, Ashley? Way too late. Look how cramped you are against the wall. And when you push off here –' Coach Vanessa paused the footage at the point where Ashley was pushing off the wall. 'See how your body pushes down into the water instead of across? That's because you were too cramped in the turn. Actually, Annabel, have a look because I noticed in the last swim comp that you do this too.'

'I do not!' retorted Annabel, offended.

'Yes, you did exactly this in the relay heats.'

Annabel reddened, then shook her head. 'Yeah, okay, let's see,' she said sheepishly.

We continued to train our tumble turns then did a light warm-down. After we'd finished in the pool, I dried myself on the deck and began stretching with my friends.

'Big session!' Ava puffed.

I laughed. 'Awesome, though.'

'I'm stuffed,' Bec whined, collapsing onto the deck.

'I'll tell you who else is stuffed,' I said arrogantly, 'the Ogilvy girls. You know, the more I train with them, the less intimidated I am by them.'

Melissa started waving her hands silently in front of me.

'What? It's true! They are meant to be the best and I just don't reckon they are as good as everybody says,' I continued loudly.

Ava and Bec joined in, waving their hands rapidly in front of their faces. I was so confused. What were they on about?

'Is that so?' a cold voice said from behind me.

I turned and saw the Ogilvy twins standing there, listening to everything I'd just said. My heart sank into my stomach. This was typical of me. Dad always said I had terminal foot-in-mouth disease.

'Oh, sorry, I didn't see you there,' I mumbled. 'I didn't mean to offend you – I mean, I was just saying that you guys are so awesome in competitions . . . Um, I guess it's kind of a compliment when I say you're not good in training. I mean, not that you're not good . . .' The words tumbled out of my mouth without me being able to control them at all.

'Ugh, dig up,' Ava mumbled, hiding a smile.

'Save it, Delphie,' one of the twins snapped. 'You're just jealous because I win everything and you are trying to pick holes in our training.'

'Yeah,' agreed the other meekly.

'Well, Ashley and I will show you,' Annabel hissed. 'We challenge you to a race. This afternoon.'

'You're on!' I said, standing tall. I loved a challenge.

'At the lake in free time. We'll race to the buoy in the centre of the lake and back again. Winner takes all bragging rights, plus the loser has to do all their kitchen duties for the rest of the week.'

'The lake?' Melissa said, frowning. 'It's out of bounds. If you get caught, you'll be banned from the carnival at the end of the week!'

'I'm not scared!' Annabel retorted. 'Are you, Delphie?'

I could feel my face reddening and my pulse beating in my ears. I hated being called scared. 'You're on!' I yelled back.

Melissa cringed. 'Oh, Delphie, no.'

'See you at the lake this afternoon, two o'clock,' I said.

Annabel and Ashley smiled and walked off.

'What were you thinking?' Bec asked. 'Don't do it. You're going to get yourself into so much trouble!'

'Delphie, you *always* do this,' Melissa added. 'Why can't you just back down sometimes?'

I shook my head. There was energy pumping through my veins. 'Because I *don't* back down,' I said flatly. 'I want to win.'

'Win in the pool, then, not in the lake!' Ava said, shaking her head.

'A challenge is a challenge,' I said stubbornly.

My friends exchanged worried glances.

'Come on, let's go,' I snapped. I hated it when my friends didn't support me. I mean, sure, the lake was out of bounds, but what was I supposed to do? Chicken out? Let the twins win? No way. If someone challenges Delphie, Delphie will meet that challenge. And Delphie *will* win.

Chapter Six

I crept down the dirt track, wildly looking from side to side. Why was I doing this? If I was caught, I was dead meat.

A kookaburra cackled, startling me. I breathed in deeply – the smell of the Australian bush was such a comforting aroma. Even though it was midwinter, the sun sparkled in the blue sky, warming me through my tracksuit top.

I broke through the bushland and into

a clearing. Dark, dirty sand fringed the expansive, muddy lake. While it wasn't a glistening ocean, it was still incredibly beautiful. The water was completely calm – a glass sheet stretching out to the horizon.

I searched around and couldn't see anyone. I took off my shoes and walked along the banks of the lake. An old, wooden jetty jutted out into the water, and in the distance I could see a buoy bobbing carelessly in the sunshine. It was a long way away.

I walked to the end of the jetty and gently sat down. I took off my tracksuit top and shorts and dumped them in a bundle on the decaying wooden deck. I slipped into the lake, feet first, to check the depth. Even with my goggles on, I could barely see anything in the muddy water. I dived down, swimming as deep as I could until I touched the soggy bottom. It was definitely deep enough to dive into. I pulled myself out of the lake and sat on the jetty, waiting for my competitors to arrive.

The winter sun was strong and warm, making the droplets of water glisten against my skin. I stretched out lazily on my back and soaked in the rays, gently closing my eyes and listening to the melodic call of the butcherbirds.

It seemed like I was lying there, still, for eternity. I sat up, puzzled, and looked at my watch. Ten past two. Maybe the twins weren't coming. Perhaps this was another stupid trick. I hoisted myself to my feet and wrapped my towel around my waist. I angrily gathered my clothes and got ready to leave.

'Chickening out?' a snide voice remarked. Walking down the jetty were the two Ogilvy girls, their arms linked.

'No way,' I retorted. 'I've checked the water depth already and it's deep enough to dive.'

The twins nodded.

'So, what are the rules?' I asked nervously.

'Swim out to the buoy, tag it and swim back. First one back to the jetty wins,' Ashley said.

I nodded.

The twins took off their tracksuits and put on their goggles. They were tall girls – a good head taller than me. Their matching dark hair was pulled back into tight ponytails.

The three of us lined up across the edge of the jetty, our toes lightly curling over the wooden edge.

'Take your mark,' the twins boomed, 'get set . . .'

'GO!'

I burst from the jetty, stretching my body into a long dive. The water crashed around my head as I broke the surface. I could immediately taste the difference from the pool – there was no scent of chlorine and some gritty droplets stuck to my lips.

I could feel the twins swimming powerfully beside me as I kicked ferociously. One twin was definitely ahead. I assumed it was Annabel, as she was the stronger freestyle swimmer of the two.

I continued with long, sleek strokes, my feet propelling me through the murky water. As I counted my breaths and strokes, I realised just how far out the buoy was. It was definitely further away than a standard fifty-metre pool. I powered on.

Finally, I reached the buoy and slapped it hard with my hand. I could glimpse one of the twins ahead of me and the other still finishing the first lap. I was in the middle – it was time to turn on the sprint.

I clenched my teeth and tried to pick up the pace after my awkward turn on the buoy. My strokes were strong and my legs kicked furiously. My eyes flicked ahead of me, gauging how close I was to the end. I could see the wooden jetty about twenty metres away. I summoned every ounce of my energy to power through.

I could feel one twin ahead of me – her toes were almost within reach. I had to win. I took huge, gasping breaths, trying to fuel myself with extra energy to overtake her.

But I didn't.

I reached the jetty, exhausted, only to see one of the twins just a half-second in front. She had won. Again.

'Champion, Annabel!' she cheered loudly. Annabel climbed up the side of the jetty, collapsing onto the deck.

A faint whistle sounded in the distance.

'Oh no, that's the coach's whistle – we've got to get out of here!' I said, hurriedly gathering my clothes.

Annabel gathered her pile and began to jog up the jetty. 'Enjoy doing my kitchen duties tonight!' She laughed mockingly. 'Ash, I'll see you back at the cabin!' she yelled over her shoulder as she tore off into the bushland.

I shook my head angrily and turned back towards the lake. There, bobbing in the distance, was Ashley. I squinted – why was she so far behind? She seemed to be treading water. Her head bobbed under the surface and back up again. She seemed frantic.

I walked to the end of the jetty and looked closer as her head bobbed back underwater. She was in trouble. 'Annabel! Help!' I screamed. But Annabel would have been halfway back to the cabins by now. There was no way she knew her sister was in danger.

I threw my clothes down and launched myself into the lake. I shook off my exhaustion from the race and tried to find some energy left in my body. I kept my eyes ahead, focusing on where Ashley was in the lake. *Hold on, Ashley. Don't go under.*

Her head continued to dip under the water and resurface. I kept her in my line of sight as I swam towards her. I finally reached her and gasped, 'Are you okay?'

'Cramp!' she spluttered.

'Turn onto your back,' I instructed, as I trod water beside her.

Ashley turned and floated on her back. I hooked my arms under her armpits and began to tow her back towards the jetty. I felt every muscle in my body screaming.

Just a little further.

I breathed hard with each kick, being sure I was keeping Ashley's face out of the water.

Just a little further.

The distance to the side of the lake was shorter than the distance back to the jetty, so I swam with Ashley to the sandy banks. I dragged her body out of the lake and we collapsed on the shore, gasping for air.

For a while, neither of us said a thing. We both panted and winced, sucking the cool air into our lungs.

Finally, Ashley sat halfway up and turned to me. 'Thank you, Delphie. Thank you.'

I nodded, still catching my breath. 'What happened out there?'

'Leg cramp. I just couldn't kick anymore. I thought I was going to drown when I saw you and Annabel running off.'

'Luckily, I looked back,' I said.

We sat there in silence, still too exhausted to stand.

'We've missed the whistle,' I said flatly.

'Don't worry, I'll cover for you. We'll tell them I had a fall and you were helping me,' Ashley said. 'I told Annabel this was a stupid idea. But she always has these grand plans that I seem to get swept along with.'

'I seem to sweep myself along with stupid, grand plans,' I said remorsefully.

'By the way, I don't think you're going to be doing kitchen duties.' Ashley laughed. 'I mean, you just saved my life. I think I owe *you* now!'

I smiled. 'Do you like being a twin?'

'I do,' Ashley said slowly. 'Having a best friend by your side all the time is amazing. But sometimes it can be hard being the … the quieter twin. Annabel does tend to dominate and sometimes I feel a little … a little lost.'

'Like you don't have a say?'

'Yeah, that's it. It's always Annabel's plans

and never mine. And I'm not brave enough to say what I think, you know?'

I laughed. 'Actually, I don't know that feeling! I reckon I'm more like your sister – act now, think later. It's not the best characteristic.'

Ashley laughed.

'Let's get back,' I said, standing up and dusting the dirty sand from my legs.

Ashley began to stand, but I could tell her legs were weak. I supported her arm as she staggered to her feet.

'Thanks – still a little wobbly,' she said, embarrassed.

'Hey, you've got a birthmark just like mine!' I said, lightening the mood. I pointed to Ashley's upper thigh where a dark brown shape peeked out from the side of her swimsuit. I turned sideways and pointed to my birthmark, which was remarkably like Ashley's.

'Mine's in the shape of a heart,' she said, outlining the heart shape with her finger.

I giggled. 'Mine's just a blob.'

I linked my arm through Ashley's to support her a bit better. She walked slowly along the side of the lake with me as we headed back to the jetty to get our gear.

'Delphie?'

'Yeah?'

'Thank you. I mean really, thank you.'

I nodded and smiled. 'No sweat.'

CHAPTER Seven

We walked down the path, which was lit up by little lights, snaking along the edge of the grass. The winter night air was cool and crisp and the stars sparkled brightly in the dark sky. I pulled my hood up over my head, the warm fleece brushing against my ears.

As we entered the hall, we were met with the buzzing sound of excited chatter. We had been told to dress warm and bring our torches with us.

'Maybe it's a "Host a Murder" night!' Ava said excitedly.

'Hide-and-seek in the dark?' Melissa asked.

'Maybe an outdoor dance party!' Bec exclaimed.

Everyone had been training really hard for the first half of camp and the coaches said we could be rewarded with a surprise fun night. We'd been speculating all afternoon about what awaited us.

'Okay, everyone, quiet!' a voice boomed from the front. It was Coach Matt. 'I'm sure you're all very anxious to hear what it is we are doing tonight …'

The noise in the room rose as everyone began guessing again.

Coach Matt held his hands up for silence. 'So, here it is. On behalf of the coaching staff, welcome to …'

All the girls drummed the floor with their hands, creating a deafening drum roll.

'… the Scavenger Hunt!'

I looked at my friends, puzzled. What on earth was a Scavenger Hunt?

Coach Vanessa stepped up. 'We've designed a whole set of clues, and in groups you have to follow the clues to the different points around the camp site and collect an item from each point. Once you have solved the clues and gathered each and every item on the list, return to the hall with your group. First team back with a completed list will win ...'

Coach Vanessa walked to the table behind her. Sitting on the table was an object that was covered in a white sheet. She lifted the sheet dramatically and revealed a massive jar filled with colourful jelly beans. Everyone cheered.

'Do we get to pick our own teams?' I yelled out hopefully.

'Thanks for raising your hand, Delphie,' Coach Stuart said sarcastically. My cheeks reddened in embarrassment. 'The answer to that is no, actually. We've mixed you up so that you are working with people from the other swim clubs. It'll be a fun way to get to know one another a bit better outside of the pool.'

'So here are the teams,' Coach Matt said, as he lifted up a piece of paper. He read through the first few teams then got to team number five. 'Team Five is Ashley Ogilvy, Madeleine Roberts, Alice Chua and Delphie Attkinson.'

I swivelled around and saw the twins sitting behind me. Hearing that we were on the same team, the one who was obviously Ashley winked at me and smiled.

'Okay, find your teammates and get moving!' Coach Stuart boomed. Immediately, the girls all leapt to their feet and chaos ensued as everyone tried to remember who was in each group.

I leapt on top of a chair, stood tall and yelled, 'My group, over here!' Sure, it was completely over the top but it worked! My group gathered quickly and we opened the paper which revealed four clues. 'Right,' I said, smoothing out the piece of paper on the floor. The others sat down around me as we decided which clue to tackle first.

'I reckon we start in the middle,' Ashley said thoughtfully. 'I bet most other groups will be starting at the top or bottom.'

I smiled. 'Good plan!'

'So, what's clue number three?' Alice asked.

Maddie, another girl in our group, picked up the paper and read aloud.

'The prize is high, way up above;

In the place where nobody wants love.'

We all frowned. It was tricky.

'In the place where nobody wants love?' I blurted. 'What the heck does that mean?'

'Well, it's got to be something to do with sport. I mean, all the places here are sport-related,' Ashley said. I could see her mind ticking over.

'But we all love our sports,' Alice said, frowning.

‘But it says you *don’t* want love,’ Maddie added.

‘Then it’s got to be hockey!’ I laughed. ‘I don’t love hockey!’

‘Love . . .’ Ashley mused. ‘Which sport has . . . I got it!’ she yelled. The group stared at her expectantly. ‘It’s tennis! Love in tennis means you have no score – you know, like, 30–Love. It means zero! You don’t want love in tennis!’

‘Genius!’ I squealed. ‘To the tennis courts!’

The four in our group leapt to our feet and turned on our torches. We followed the path down past the dining hall and over to the indoor and outdoor tennis courts. The indoor courts were locked, so it had to be on one of the outdoor courts. Ashley’s idea to start in the middle had definitely paid off. There were no other groups on the tennis courts and we were able to hunt around freely.

‘It said “high up above”,’ said Alice, scanning the court. ‘There!’ she said, pointing to the tall umpire’s chair.

I scaled the umpire's chair, and there, sitting on the top of the seat, was a basket filled with the items the groups needed to collect to return to the hall. In this case, it was a tennis ball. I threw the ball down to Maddie and she put it into her backpack, which we'd brought along with us.

'Done! Right, what's next?' Maddie asked, sitting down on the court.

We huddled around Alice, who was holding all the clues. 'How about we try number four, now?' Alice suggested. We nodded in agreement. 'Here it is,' she said, clearing her voice.

'*Catch the ball, but be sure to stop!*
Score a goal and your prize will drop.'

'Let's think about this. Which sports use balls?' Alice asked, folding the piece of paper into her pocket.

'Soccer, softball, netball, basketball, hockey – we'll be running all over the campus if we don't narrow it down!' Maddie moaned.

'It says you need to score a goal, so that rules out softball,' I said.

'Okay, let me think,' Ashley said slowly. I could see her mind whirring away as she recited the clue to herself. In the light of the torch, I noticed her face was narrow as she mouthed the words. She definitely had a slimmer face than her sister, which I'd never realised before. 'You have to stop. The only sport where you can't move when you have the ball is … is … netball!' she said, looking up with bright eyes.

'Gold!' I yelled, giving her a quick hug. 'To the netball courts!'

We bolted back through the campus and over to the netball courts. The courts were inside, the doors were unlocked and the lights on. There were several netball hoops set up for shooting practice. We scanned the gym and began running around, looking in the stalls and on the ground.

'Hey, up there!' Alice yelled.

We all looked and there, in the hoop she was pointing to, was a package wrapped in brown paper. It was wedged into the netball ring. There were also similar packages wedged into other hoops.

'How on earth are we going to get that down?' Alice panted.

'Maybe there's a stick or a cleaner's mop,' I said, searching around the room.

'Wait, get the clue out again,' Ashley said.

Alice pulled the clue out and read it again.

'Catch the ball, but be sure to stop!

Score a goal and your prize will drop.'

'Score a goal – we have to use the ball to knock it out of the goal!' Ashley exclaimed. She pointed to a big box sitting on the sidelines of the court. Sure enough, the box was filled with netballs.

'I'll have a go!' I yelled excitedly, as I grabbed a ball. The others followed me and we formed a line in front of the hoop. We each had a turn at shooting, all of us missing hopelessly.

Maddie laughed. 'Swimmers might not have the most awesome hand-eye coordination.'

We each took another shot and finally Alice got lucky with her ball skittering into the hoop. As her ball pushed through, the brown package was dislodged and it fell to the ground lightly. It clearly wasn't a heavy item. We ran over to where the package had landed. I picked it up and unwrapped several layers of paper until I revealed a netball bib, which was neatly folded into a square.

'Right, done,' I said, throwing Maddie the bib to put in her bag. 'We are smashing this!'

Another group entered the hall and began looking around the gym, trying to solve the clue we had just completed. I noticed immediately that one of the people in the group was Annabel.

'How many have you got?' Ashley yelled out to her sister.

'Sorry, classified information!' Annabel said, raising her eyebrows. Ashley poked her tongue out at her sister and they smiled at each other.

'Hey, you've got a dimple in your cheek!' I said to Ashley. 'And Annabel doesn't! I'd never noticed it before.'

Annabel glared at me, irritated.

'Yep, we're not *completely* identical,' Ashley laughed. But Annabel shot her an angry glance and shook her head aggressively. Ashley's smile disappeared. She looked down and said, 'Let's get to the next clue.'

'What's your sister's problem?' I whispered.

Ashley shrugged her shoulders and gestured to Alice to get out the clue sheet again.

Alice read clue number one:

'Chalk it up, go for a swing;

Perfect scores will help you win.'

'Swing. Is there a park somewhere on the camp site?' I asked.

'But there's chalk,' Maddie pointed out. 'Weightlifting? They use chalk.'

'No, it's gymnastics,' Ashley said simply. 'You swing on the bar and use chalk on your hands. And they are aiming for perfect scores to win.'

We stared down at the page. It seemed so obvious now!

'Ashley, were you some kind of FBI agent in a former life?' Alice joked.

Ashley smiled as we ran out of the netball courts and down to the gymnasium where the gymnastics equipment was set up. We entered the gym and it was huge.

'This is like looking for a needle in a haystack!' Maddie yelled. 'Look at that foam pit. What if it's in there?'

We looked towards the sea of foam cubes sitting under a high metal bar.

'Well, the clue did say to "chalk it up", so I reckon we start at the bars,' Alice said.

We all nodded and headed over to the sets of bars. We hunted around the mats and on top of the bars but couldn't see anything.

'What about *in* the chalk?' Maddie asked. 'It said "chalk it up", maybe it's in the bucket.'

Along the wall, there were several different buckets of chalk. I walked over to one and slid my hands into the soft, powdery chalk. As I felt about, light puffs of chalk rose into the air. I coughed and spluttered a little. After a few seconds, my fingers felt something – it was soft and long. I pulled out a thin, blue ribbon. 'This is it! Only one more to go!' I yelled triumphantly. I could almost taste those jelly beans. I dusted off the ribbon and put it in Maddie's bag.

Alice passed the paper to Maddie, who read the next clue.

'Stretch out long, go out, not up;
Buried treasure in a sandy lot.'

We all immediately turned to Ashley. She had been our Sherlock Holmes so far and we needed her to get this final clue.

'Stretch out, not up,' she said slowly. 'Well, every sport requires stretching. Help me out here!' She laughed.

'Maybe the prize is in sand. It does say "sandy lot",' Alice said.

'Beach volleyball?' Maddie asked.

'I don't think there is a beach volleyball court here,' Alice replied.

'Where else is there sand?' I asked.

'I got it!' Ashley yelled. Detective Ashley strikes again. 'Go out, not up. Go long, not high. It's long jump. Long jump into a sandy pit!'

We bolted along the path, the light of our torches bouncing along in front of us. The track and field area was all the way down the other side of the camp and we knew we had to get there fast if we were going to win this thing.

We arrived at the long jump pit and saw there were several holes already dug into the sand.

'Okay, some of the other teams have found their prizes. We need to dig fast to find ours,' Alice said.

We launched ourselves into the pit, digging frantically. Sand tossed about in the air, raining down into my hair.

'The other holes are quite deep. I reckon ours will be deep too,' Ashley said logically.

We continued to dig around like puppies on the beach, searching in a desperate frenzy. Suddenly, my fingers scraped against something hard.

'I think I've got it!'

The others raced over to help me. It was a small wooden box. We lifted it onto my lap and I gently opened the latch. Inside was a glistening gold medal. We all smiled. As athletes, there was one thing each of us understood. And that was the rush that came with holding a cold, shining medal between our fingers.

With our items safely packed in Maddie's bag, we ran back to the hall as quickly as we could. But as we approached the hall, we saw Annabel's group also running towards the entrance. They must have finished the hunt too.

'Quick!' Annabel yelled. 'It's another group! Let's GO!' She ran ahead of her team with a look of fierce determination in her eyes.

We turned on the pace, desperate to beat them. As we approached the door, Annabel began to sprint. She ran past my group, pulled Ashley back out of the doorway and pushed in front of her.

'Hey!' Ashley shouted.

'I win!' Annabel yelled, as she slapped her hand on the coach's table.

Our group ran in behind her and gathered around the coaches. The rest of Annabel's team ran in after us.

'Sorry, Annabel,' Coach Vanessa said, shaking her head. 'I specifically said it was the first *team* to get back, not the first person. Delphie's is the first to get back together, so we'll check their items off first.'

Annabel huffed angrily and sat down on the floor.

Coach Stuart checked each of our items.

'Tennis ball, bib, ribbon and medal. You got it, girls!'

My team jumped up and down as we hugged each other. Coach Matt blew a loud whistle, signalling to the remaining teams that the game was over and they needed to come back.

As all the teams gathered in the hall, Coach Vanessa presented our team with the jar of jelly beans. 'Well done, you guys!' she said, as everyone applauded.

'Couldn't have done it without our very own Sherlock Holmes!' I said, handing the jar to Ashley. She looked slightly taken aback. But then she smiled and lifted the jelly beans high into the air with everybody cheering around her.

I scanned the room, seeing the bright, happy faces whistling and cheering for Ashley. Everyone, that is, except for one person. Annabel sat still, with a cold face, and her hands neatly folded in her lap. I knew in that moment that she was going to give it everything she had in the pool. Annabel did not like to lose.

'Oooh, I just love yoga,' Melissa said, shaking out her legs.

'So good after a full week of swimming. My muscles were so tight and now I feel super relaxed and ready for the carnival!' Ava said.

We lifted our yoga mats and dragged them back over to the pile in the corner of the studio. We grabbed our shoes and took a drink from our water bottles.

'I can't wait for the carnival,' I gushed.

'I feel like I've really improved my swimming this week – especially my turns. I can just feel a win coming up in the relay this time!'

'So, what's the deal with today?' Bec asked.

'Coach Stuart said we are going to do a run-through of our races for tomorrow. Then we have a free afternoon!' Ava replied.

We strolled back up to the aquatic centre. Yoga had a way of calming us all down, which was a good thing in my case. My mind was always overwhelmed with thoughts, so it was nice to be able to slow down sometimes.

We entered the aquatic centre and walked up to the change rooms. We were early so didn't think anyone else was in there yet. As we walked through the door, we were met with a hushed but angry conversation between two people.

'It's just a few practice races today. You'll be *fine*,' one voice said.

'I don't want to exhaust myself before tomorrow, though,' the other hissed angrily.

'Yeah, well, maybe I don't want to be exhausted either, but that's life,' the other snapped.

We rounded the corner to see the Ogilvy twins in a heated discussion.

Annabel's head snapped up. 'What are you looking at?' she sneered.

Suddenly, I realised something. I knew it was Annabel. Usually, I had to wait for one of them to tell me who it was, but this time I knew immediately.

With the girls gathered by the side of the pool, our coaches called us all into our swim schools for a pep talk. Coach Stuart decided to take our team outside onto the outdoor deck. The winter sun was warm on our faces as we sat in a circle with Coach Stuart in the middle.

'Today we are going to do some practice races with the other clubs to get ready for the comp tomorrow. I don't want you working your hardest, do you understand? Take it easy. This is just to go through your race formats and get into the competitive mindset. Keep something in the tank for tomorrow.'

We each nodded excitedly. The carnival was going to be a really good test for us. State trials were just around the corner and this meet would give us a solid indication as to who would be going. Plus, there were those beautiful medals to win.

'Delphie, can I have a word?' Coach Stuart asked. I walked over to him as the rest of the girls headed back to the pool. 'Now, you know I consider you to be a bit of a team captain among the girls in the squad.' I blushed lightly – I loved that he gave me added responsibility. 'I need you to fire up the girls like you always do. Especially your relay team.'

'Of course!' I beamed.

'But, I also need you to … you know … keep your head screwed on.'

'What do you mean?' I asked, a bit defensively.

'I'm just saying I need you to be level-headed. Don't do anything brash or crazy.'

'I don't act crazy!'

'You know what I mean. Remember to think before you act. I know you'll do great.' Coach Stuart patted me lightly on the shoulder as I walked back into the aquatic centre.

I had four events to swim in the carnival, which meant four warm-up races today. Tomorrow we had to swim each event in both heats and finals – it was a much busier day than just running through the events once.

Towards the end of training, we got ready to swim through our mixed medley relay. It was my favourite race and a great chance for some teamwork with my best friends. I gathered the girls together for a pre-swim psych-up.

'Now, girls, remember to leave something in the tank. This is just a practice, but tomorrow we have to swim both the heat and the final. This is our chance to show the National Swim School who we really are, yeah?'

Bec, Ava and Melissa nodded.

'They always seem to swim slower in heats and training anyway,' Bec said. 'I think it's part of their game plan.'

'Well, whatever their plan is, ours is to win tomorrow. So let's work well together today and then smash it out in the finals tomorrow!'

The girls gave a whoop as we readied ourselves for a run-through of the medley.

Melissa eased herself into the pool and got into position, ready to launch into her backstroke leg. Coach Vanessa blew her whistle and Melissa launched powerfully into the water. Her body undulated through the water before breaking the surface in a frenzied backstroke. I could see her technique had improved in the five days at training camp.

Melissa held the lead as she glided through the last lap of her backstroke. Once she finished, Bec launched into her breaststroke. She bobbed up and down at a cracking pace, maintaining our lead over the Swim School. I knew that this was just a practice, but I'll admit, it felt awesome being in the lead. We just had to replicate it tomorrow.

As Bec finished her leg, Ava was readying herself for the butterfly. Right on cue, Ava burst from the blocks into a soaring dive. As she pulsed through the water, her shoulder muscles flexed and rotated. She was amazing to watch. She lengthened our lead, with the Swim School in second place.

Now, it was all down to me. I stood on the blocks, shaking out my arms and legs. Despite it being a practice, energy pulsed through my veins. It was like my body could not get the message that this wasn't the real thing.

As Ava neared the end of her lap, I glanced quickly to my left to see Annabel Ogilvy ready to dive. She quickly glanced back at me … and then it happened.

She smiled lightly.

She smiled at me. Her face was narrow and I saw the hint of a dimple. I frowned in confusion. My eyes dropped down to her legs. There, poking out from her swimmers was a heart-shaped birthmark. At that moment it dawned on me. I wasn't looking at Annabel. I was looking at Ashley.

'Delphie, go!' a voice boomed from behind me.

I was startled. I'd completely missed my cue. I dived into the water as a confused Ava hauled herself out of the pool.

Why was Ashley swimming in the relay today?

A host of images and sounds swept through my mind as I swam. Coach Vanessa had said Annabel had done a faulty tumble turn 'just like Ashley does' in the last meet's heats. Annabel said she got exhausted quickly. The Swim School never qualified as fast in heats. But they always won the finals. Ashley was always getting swept up in Annabel's plans, or so she said. But what about the birthmark? We usually wore knee-length skins in competitions too. I had no chance of seeing the birthmark before.

My mind raced.

BANG!

I stood up in the shallow end and shook my head in confusion. What had happened?

'Delphie, are you all right?' Coach Stuart's voice called down to me.

I rubbed my head and nodded in confusion. Had I just swum into the wall? I looked behind me and saw the others had finished the race down the other end. I felt so confused.

'Pull her out,' I heard Coach Stuart say.

I felt sick and a little dizzy. I sat down at the end of the pool as people began to gather around.

'What happened?' Ava said, crouching down next to me. 'You just swam full pace into the wall!'

'Did I?' I glanced up, dizzy and confused. In the distance I could see the Ogilvy twins tiptoeing up the stairs back to the change rooms. The one with the birthmark was wet from swimming in my race. I shook my head. It was definitely Ashley.

Just like when the last piece of a 1000-piece jigsaw falls into place, the picture became crystal clear. Ashley had been swimming the heats for Annabel. That's how Annabel still had loads of energy for the finals. She'd been resting while her twin swam her heats.

I felt like my blood was boiling. How could they do this? How could they cheat? I thought Ashley had become my friend! Everything in me wanted to jump up and scream 'Cheaters!' It was like I was going to explode. My head swam and there was a roaring sound in my ears. I wanted to cry out, but I couldn't open my mouth. And then everything went black as I fell to the floor.

CHAPTER Nine

I was gliding through the water, swimming faster than ever before. The water felt crisp and cool on my long, sleek body. I glanced back and saw my silver tail, pulsing in the water, propelling me forwards. I was a dolphin. I smiled brightly. With a rush of energy, I gracefully moved my tail faster through the water as I gathered speed. I gazed above me and could see the sun dancing on the surface of the water. I twisted in a 360-degree spin, corkscrewing through the waves. With a swish of my tail, I gathered speed as I headed up to the surface. With one final, powerful thump of my tail, I launched myself up, out of the water. As I broke the surface, the bright light of day burst all around me, lighting me up like glistening silver glass. I kicked with glee as I soared like a bird above the water. Then my body became heavier and I crashed back down into the waves – back into my domain of the sea.

As I swam, I suddenly felt a presence. The waters seemed to turn dark. I twisted to see what was lurking beneath. A shadow. I turned sharply, ready to swim back to the safety of my pod. But the shadow rose underneath me. Panic rushed through me. I turned again to see the shadow gain speed. I pushed my body as hard as I could.

Just swim. Just a little further.

I could practically feel the jaws of my predator open behind me, engulfing my tail.

I became frantic. The huge shadow of my pursuer dwarfed me. In pure fear and panic, I looked back – I wanted to see it. And there behind me was a monster of the sea. Its mouth was a gaping hole with razor-sharp, shining teeth. Its eyes were completely black – it was like looking into a bottomless pit. I tried to squeal but no sound came out.

The monster's head turned sharply. It seemed bothered. It tried to turn back towards me but it was as if something was dragging its head sideways, jolting and jarring it. I swallowed my fear.

In one aggressive pull, the monster's head was yanked roughly to the side, causing it to twist and writhe. The monster gave up. As it turned to swim away, I saw that it had no tail. At the base of its body, in place of its tail, was another monstrous head. But this head had its mouth tightly closed, with no murderous intent. Its eyes were not black but blue, like the sea. It was the back half of the monster that had been pulling the head of terror away from me.

The monstrous creature swam away. All I could see was the back end of it – the head that had saved me – staring at me sadly as it disappeared into the dark.

I sat up in bed with a jolt. That was so weird. I rubbed my head where it was still tender from my accident that day. I thought back to training – to fainting on the side of the pool. I'd been taken to the camp nurse and she had cleared me for the swimming competition the next day. She said it was only a light bump and that I should take it easy for the rest of the day. I'd come back to my room for a rest while the others finished training.

My mind abruptly caught up with my situation as I remembered my terrible discovery. The Ogilvy twins. The cheaters.

I've got to report them.

As I stood up, a fresh pain throbbed in my head. I pulled on my tracksuit pants and began for the door. I had to tell the coaching staff and officials. These girls needed to be thrown out of the competition. But then I thought of Ashley.

I frowned. I thought she was my friend. But she couldn't be. Friends didn't lie and cheat. I jiggled nervously as my hand hovered over the cabin doorknob. I turned and saw my mobile phone, charging on the bedside table. I walked over and yanked out the plug, then began typing furiously, stabbing the keypad with my thumbs. I typed out the entire situation. I hit 'send'. Then I waited.

A couple of minutes later, my phone made a light *bling!* I grabbed it and opened the message.

FlyingEvie335: That is heavy, Delphie. Wot u gonna do?

It was my good friend Evie. She would know what to do.

DelphieDolphin: I want to report them.

FlyingEvie335: But you said Ashley was your friend.

DelphieDolphin: Well, I thought she was.

FlyingEvie335: Wot is holding you back from telling?

DelphieDolphin: I dunno. Maybe this time I need to stop and think and not rush into things like I usually do.

FlyingEvie335: Can u talk to them? Tell them u know. Make them answer.

I stared at my screen. Make them answer.

DelphieDolphin: Thx E. Luv u.

I sat back down on my bed. This was big. This could ruin everything for the twins. I needed to go against everything I normally did, I had to stop and think.

As I mulled over my options, I heard footsteps coming towards the cabin. I jumped up and pulled the curtains by the front door open just a slither. Coming towards the cabin were Ashley and Annabel, arm in arm. They looked concerned, like they were having a serious conversation. I watched them as they walked into their cabin.

I took a deep breath and opened my door. I looked to my left – back up to the main part of the camp site, where the coaches awaited my report. I looked to my right to the Ogilvy girls' cabin. I paused and closed my eyes.

Then I turned right.

CHAPTER Ten

I banged on the door furiously, my hands shaking.

The door opened.

'Delphie, are you okay?'

'I know everything, Ashley.' Ashley's face went pale and I saw Annabel stand up behind her. 'Let me in, otherwise I'm walking straight up to the coaches' lounge.' Annabel sat back down as I entered their cabin. 'Notice how I knew who answered the door?' I said, trying to keep my voice from shaking. 'I can tell you apart, you know. And I know Ashley swam against me in the medley.'

'Oh, come on, Delphie,' Annabel said in a light voice. 'Everyone mixes us up. We're *twins*. You made a silly mistake!'

'I didn't. I know your faces because Ashley is ... *was* my friend. And I saw her birthmark. She has one on her leg and you don't. Even if I made a mistake with your faces, you can't mistake a birthmark.'

Annabel's eyes widened in panic. She looked to Ashley, who shrugged her shoulders. They knew they couldn't fight this one.

'It's not a big deal, Delphie,' Annabel muttered. 'I swim the final – the race that matters. And that's the race we win.'

'Only because you don't swim any heats over the entire day! You swim half the races I do. You can't say that's not an advantage, Annabel!' I spat. 'And what about your sister? She gets to swim all her heats *and* yours?

How do you think she feels at the end of the day?'

'She doesn't care,' Annabel yelled, 'because she never wins anyway!'

Ashley glared at her sister. 'Who knows? I might win if I had the chance!'

Annabel scowled. 'Oh, Ashley, you've always been the inferior swimmer and you know it.'

'Well, not anymore. I'm not doing this for you ever again. You can swim your own stupid races from now on.'

'You two are so dramatic!' Annabel said with a sarcastic laugh. 'In the Olympics you are *allowed* to use different swimmers in the heats and finals in a mixed relay. It's completely legal!'

'But we aren't in the Olympics, Annabel,' I yelled. 'In our region, you have to keep the same team. It's in the rules. And what about the other individual races that you're always winning? Is Ashley swimming those heats too? Because that's illegal in every swimming meet in the world!'

Tears broke from Ashley's eyes and ran down her face.

'So, what are you going to do, Delphie? If you report me, you are also incriminating Ashley. You are betraying your new *friend*,' Annabel sneered.

Ashley searched my face with pleading eyes. 'Please, give us a chance,' she whispered.

'You know,' I said slowly, lowering the volume of my voice, 'my usual hot-headed self would have reported you within seconds of finding this out.'

Annabel's eyes widened.

'But I'm going to do something completely different and I'm going to wait. I'm going to wait and watch. I'm going to give you two the chance to redeem yourselves. You swim tomorrow, but you swim as *yourselves*.'

Gratitude washed over Ashley's face. She leapt to her feet and hugged me tightly. 'Thank you,' she whispered.

'But I will be watching closely. You know

that I can tell you apart. And from now on, I will be at every swim meet you race in. We swim in the same region and we will probably swim at state on the same team. Who knows, one day we might even swim together for our country, so I will be watching. And I will end your careers if I ever catch you cheating again.'

Annabel breathed out, clearly relieved.

'Tomorrow, in the pool, we'll see who the best is,' I said then turned and walked out of the cabin, slamming the door behind me.

On the porch outside, I squatted down on the floor. I breathed heavily, panting as if I'd just swum the race of my life. I coughed lightly and swallowed hard, clinging to the ground for balance. I knew that was the most composed I'd ever been in my life. I'd kept hot-headed Delphie under control and I think I'd done the right thing.

Now I knew I needed to swim the race of my life tomorrow and prove to Annabel that cheaters don't win. I had to swim with all my strength and leave nothing in the tank. Everything came down to that final race. I had to swim like a dolphin. And win.

CHAPTER Eleven

I tapped my finger on my smart phone, selecting my pre-carnival playlist. It was psych-up time. I popped the headphones in my ears and slung my bag over my shoulder. As I exited my cabin, I could see it was a sunny, crisp winter's day. I pulled my hoodie over my head, blocking out the world around me and focusing on my music.

I'd seen my friends that morning over breakfast, but the mood was pretty quiet in the dining hall. Everyone had their own way of psyching themselves up before a meet and mine was to block out everything around me and focus. I did this by listening to my favourite up-beat tracks on my phone. I breathed in deeply as I slowly walked up to the aquatic centre. In my head, I rehearsed my races – both individual races and the medley.

I wonder what the twins will …

STOP!

I couldn't think about the twins now. I had to concentrate.

I entered the aquatic centre and it was alive with the hum of nerves. I found the marshalling table and checked out the order of my races. Since it was a one-day meet, the heats and finals were pretty close together. This was exactly the kind of meet where Annabel would want someone else to swim her heats. But not today.

In the change rooms, most of the girls were quiet and focused. There were a few who were giggling nervously and being silly, but

I tuned them out as I unpacked my bag. I had my competition skins on – a knee-length swimsuit in the Academy colours, as well as the goggles and cap that I kept for competing. They were the best quality, but I liked to think they were also lucky and a bit special.

As I left the change room, I startled as I almost bumped into someone. Looking up, I saw it was Ashley. She opened her mouth as if to say something, but I held up my hand. I couldn't deal with her right now. This was my meet and I wasn't going to be distracted by anyone. She seemed to understand, closing her mouth and lowering her head sadly.

Down by the pool, everyone began their warm-up drills. I let my body glide through the water slowly and smoothly. I wanted to get my muscles moving but still conserve my energy. I felt the flow of the water around me, noting the warm temperature and getting a feel for the pool. I know that sounds a bit weird – doesn't water always feel the same?

Funnily enough, it doesn't. I always liked getting a sense of what my body felt like in the water on that particular day. I finished my lap, lightly sailing to the end of the pool with an outstretched arm. As I lifted my head from the water, like a whale breeching for air, I heard a voice at the end of the pool calling to me. I looked up.

'Yes, Coach Stuart?'

'Hop out and come here a sec,' he said, motioning for me to follow him. I heaved myself out of the pool and walked over to him.

'Delphie, are you all right?'

'Yeah, I'm just focusing,' I said.

'I wanted to check on you. You seem quieter than normal and after you bumped your head yesterday, I just –'

'I'm honestly fine, Coach.'

'Okay, well, your heats for the 100-metre freestyle are early in the program, so make sure you are all warmed-up. Remember not to use all your energy in the heats – pull back a bit, and if you are having any problems with your head –'

'My head is fine!' I whined.

'– *any* problems, come and tell me. We can rest you from the relay if needed.'

'No way, Coach! I'm ready for this relay. It's time to take the title back for the Academy.'

Coach Stuart smiled. He knew I was as stubborn as a donkey. He patted me on the shoulder and I returned his smile.

As the carnival started, butterflies began to dance around in my stomach. A nervous and excited energy pulsed through my veins, causing me to jitter and shift around as I waited for my heat. I kept my headphones in my ears, pumping my playlist and blocking out the distractions around me.

It was almost my turn to swim the 100-metre freestyle heat. I stood in my group, quietly pulsing up and down on the spot, keeping my blood flowing. The heat before mine was also a 100-metre freestyle heat, the winner likely to go on to the final later in the day. I watched as the swimmers stood on their starting blocks. Annabel Ogilvy glanced quickly to the side and saw me watching her. She immediately looked back ahead of her, focusing on the race. Even though I couldn't see the twin's leg because of her knee-length competition skins, I could tell it was Annabel swimming her own heat – she had a rounder face than her sister and a stone-cold expression.

The electronic starter buzzed loudly as the heat began. I knew I should be ignoring Annabel's race and focusing on my own, but I couldn't help staring. Annabel burst from the block and swam at a frenzied pace. Even though it was only a heat, she charged through the water like a great white shark pursuing its prey. Her tumble turn was fast as she pushed off the wall at maximum strength.

It was perfect. She thundered through her last lap and smacked the wall with her hand, finishing the race in first position. She turned and whipped off her goggles to look at the scoreboard.

1. Annabel Ogilvy 0:58:55

Annabel turned to me and smiled. She'd qualified first in her heat with a good time.

I tried to shake off her race and focus on my own as I climbed on top of the block.

BEEP!

The starter sounded and I launched off the blocks, my body stretched out long and lean. A deafening crash thundered around my ears as I hit the water. I knew what I had to do. Focus, pace myself and leave a little in the tank for later.

I counted my strokes, trying to find a fast, even rhythm. I glided through the water at speed, although I could feel my rhythm wasn't at its best. As I approached the wall for my turn, I could tell my timing was off. I turned early and as I pushed off the wall, I realised I didn't have maximum kick-off.

I knew I had to pick up speed to make sure I qualified for the finals. Even though the heats weren't meant to be my best race, there was no point swimming so slowly that I didn't qualify for the finals at all. I propelled myself through the water, gathering speed for my final few metres. I hit the wall hard and turned to look at the scoreboard.

2. Delphine Attkinson 0:59.24

I'd come second in my heat with a time pretty far behind Annabel's. But it should be enough to make the finals. As I pulled myself out of the pool, Coach Stuart was there to meet me.

'Good race, Delph,' he said, clapping his hand on my shoulder. 'I think the tumble turn was what slowed you down there –'

'I turned too early.'

'Yep, exactly. So for the finals, make sure you get a better rhythm and focus on that turn at the end of the pool.'

I nodded as he held up his hand for a high five. I slapped his hand nonchalantly and walked slowly over to the cool-down pool. I slipped into the water, allowing it to soothe my body. It was important to cool down after a race and I always enjoyed the feeling of unwinding in the water. It gave me the chance to focus on my other races for the day, particularly the 100-metre final and the medley, which I was going to be swimming against Annabel.

I sat on the edge of the pool, gently kicking my legs against the water.

'Delphie?'

I looked up and saw Ashley standing beside me.

'Can I sit down?' she asked nervously.

I nodded.

'I just wanted to say, good swim in your heat. And, guess what?'

I looked up at her with raised eyebrows. Her eyes were shining and her little dimple was dancing on the edge of her cheek as she tried to hide a smile.

'I qualified first in my breaststroke heat!'

'That's awesome, Ashley,' I said, genuinely excited for her.

'I never qualify first. I'm always too focused on Annabel's races that I never have the mental energy for my own. I think I can actually win something today!'

I smiled at Ashley.

'Do you reckon you are going to win the 100-metre final?' she asked me quietly.

'I dunno,' I said. 'But I'm going to give it everything I have.'

Ashley nodded as she stood up. 'Good luck, Delphie. Swim fast!'

I breathed in deeply.

Swim fast.

I stood on the blocks, my legs shaking slightly. This was it. The 100-metre freestyle final. Annabel was in the centre lane and I was further towards the outer lanes, due to my slower qualifying time. I was actually pretty glad I wasn't right next to her. It meant I could focus on my own race.

I had been watching Annabel closely all day and I knew she had been swimming her own heats. For once it was a completely level playing field.

The buzzer sounded and we burst from the blocks. My start was a good one – I knew I had responded with lightning reflex. My dive was good, I pulsed my body under the water, and as I broke the surface I began my strokes. My rhythm was even. My kick was strong and my breathing was perfectly timed with my strokes.

As I approached the wall, I remembered Coach Stuart's advice. I had to time this right. With a long, outstretched arm, I reached forwards and pulled my body into a tight, tucked position. I felt my feet hit the wall in a great position, knowing it was perfect for maximum push-off. With all my strength, I launched into my final lap.

I kicked my feet hard and ramped up the pace as I approached the final few metres of my race. I propelled my body towards the end of the pool, hitting the end wall with my open palm.

It was a good race. I'd done it right and it felt fast. Had I done enough?

I turned and pulled off my goggles but kept my eyes closed. I could hear the cheers of the crowd around me – were those cheers for me?

I opened my eyes to see the scoreboard blinking back at me.

1. Annabel Ogilvy 0:58.01 (New Record)
2. Delphine Attkinson 0:58.55

I looked over to the centre lane and saw Annabel fist-pumping the air. Tears pricked my eyes. I pulled myself out of the pool, feeling like I'd been punched in the stomach.

Coach Stuart ran over. 'Delphie! Silver medal! And a personal best! High five, girl!' His face was beaming.

I couldn't even muster a smile.

'What's up?' he said, confused.

'I wanted to win. That was meant to be *my* race. It was finally a level playing field and I still lost.' I swallowed hard, trying not to let the tears flow down my cheeks.

'Level playing field – what are you talking

about? You got a personal best, Delphie – you didn't lose!'

I sniffed, shaking my head, trying to smother the wave of emotions bubbling to the surface.

Coach Stuart patted my shoulder lightly. 'Delphie, I'm so proud of you. The way you swam today and how you led our team has really impressed me. You've still got the relay to go, so you need to move on from this and focus on your next job. I need you to be the anchor for our team – to guide the other girls and get them in the right headspace. I'm relying on you.'

I nodded, feeling slightly better. Coach Stuart was right. I had one more job to do and it was to win back the mixed medley title for the Academy.

'Okay,' I said resolutely. 'Let's do this.'

CHAPTER Thirteen

'Girls, this is it. This is our time. It's time to win back that title for the Academy,' I said energetically, bouncing lightly on my toes. I could see Bec, Ava and Melissa nodding enthusiastically, feeding off my energy. This is what I did best. 'We've all swum our guts out today – some of us seven or eight races – it's been a huge day. And this is our final swim. It's time to dig deep. Find the energy that's left in the tank and use everything you've got.'

'Yeah!' Melissa yelled, pumping the air with her fist.

I looked to my left and saw the National Swim School relay team gathered in a huddle around Annabel. She was clearly giving them the same pep talk I was. They clapped their hands and slapped each other on the back.

'Mel, start us off strong, girl. You know you can do this,' I said, holding Melissa's shoulders and looking her straight in the eye. Melissa nodded and smiled. She was our backstroke swimmer and the first leg of the race.

With a bright smile, she lowered herself into the water and squatted her body up against the wall, ready to launch into her backstroke leg.

'Take your marks …'

BEEP!

'Come on, Mel!' I yelled.

The backstroke swimmers were covered in a whitewash of frenzied splashing. Melissa propelled herself through the water, her arms rotating like a windmill as she pulled her body along. She was in second place.

'Come on, Melissa!' Ava shrieked in my ear.

The crowd was on its feet – everyone gathered into their swimming clubs, cheering with all their might. I could hear the chant from the Academy girls. But over the top of it I could hear the pulse of the National Swim School girls.

Swim School! Swim School!

As Melissa neared the end of her lap, Bec stood tall, following her strokes, readying herself for the breaststroke leg. Right on cue, Bec launched herself into the water. As she broke the surface, she began bobbing up and down at great pace.

Bec was usually our weaker swimmer in the relay, but today she was on fire. She caught up to the Swim School breaststroker and, after a good turn, ended up slightly in front. Ava screamed in delight. Ava was our strongest swimmer, and if Bec could maintain the lead, Ava could certainly cement it.

As Bec finished her lap, Ava stretched out her long, muscly body in a soaring dive. Her shoulders pummelled through the water, her body thundering along at a rapid pace. She was a picture of power and beauty when she swam.

Ava approached the wall for her turn, and I began to psych myself up for my lap.

'Come on!' a voice screeched from the lane beside me. I glanced up and saw Annabel screaming at her teammate to pick up the pace. I shook my head and tried to ignore her. I had to focus on *my* race.

As Ava turned, I noticed her timing was off. This was very unusual for Ava – she was our flawless swimmer. To see her do an awkward tumble turn rattled me a bit. She pushed off the wall and the Swim School butterfly swimmer took the lead.

'Yes!' Annabel screeched.

Ava thundered towards me, I crouched down, ready to swim my lap. We were in second place and I had to bring this home. Ava reached for the wall and I burst from the blocks like a bullet from a gun. My mind focused in on the lane in front of me, completely blocking out Annabel and the crowd from my consciousness. The sound from the crowd around me faded away until all I could hear was my own breath and my arms slicing through the water.

I felt like I was gliding through air – the water around me was light and smooth. As I approached the wall for my turn, I reached out my arm and twisted my body. My two feet planted onto the wall and I burst off, using all my strength.

My body undulated in the water; I felt like a creature of the sea. I was Delphin, mythological creature, completely at one with my watery world.

I turned on the pace for my final few

metres. I knew this was my last chance to give it everything I had. I dug deep within myself to find any last scraps of energy I had. I channelled that energy into my legs and arms. This was it.

I thumped the wall with my hands and dipped my head down towards the water. I had given it my all. I could hear the crowd screaming and cheering, but I couldn't look up.

Suddenly, a hand reached down into the water. It was Melissa, beaming brightly. She was pointing at the scoreboard.

1. The Academy of Sport for Girls
2. The National Swim School

I rubbed my eyes to make sure they were free from water and looked again. Melissa, Ava and Bec were squealing with delight. I pulled myself out of the pool and embraced my teammates.

We all cheered. 'We did it! 'We did it!'

Coach Stuart ran over and high-fived us all. 'You did it!' he yelled.

We jumped up and down in a huddle, screaming with joy.

I felt a tap on my shoulder and I turned to see a face smiling at me. At first I thought it was Ashley, but then I realised this face had no dimple and was rounder in shape. It was Annabel.

'Great swim,' she said, extending her hand in a handshake.

In speechless awe, I took her hand. 'Great swim,' I echoed back.

I peered up to the gallery and saw another face, smiling and yelling. It was Ashley, waving at me. I waved back and smiled. She held up a 'number one' finger. I nodded happily and held up a 'number one' finger too.

We had done it.

CHARACTER PROFILE

Name: Delphine Attkinson (you can call me Delphie-Dolphin!)

Hair colour: White-blonde (totally natural!)

Eye colour: Blue

Bestie: Oh, I can't name just one! My swimming buddies – Ava, Melissa and Bec – and then of course Evie from school. She's a gymnast at the Academy. And also my fellow Maths-hater – Josie – she's a runner. We HATE Maths! I guess I don't have one bestie. I love everyone!

Likes: The beach; ocean swimming; surfing; running; swim training; yoga; chocolate; loud music; dancing; being the centre of attention; my noisy siblings – what can I say? I love life!

Dislikes: Maths; people who cheat; muscle cramps; swimming caps.

If I couldn't be a famous athlete, I would be ... a pop star. Or Prime Minister. I'd be a cool Prime Minister.

If I was at a party, I would be ... in the middle of the room, having a dance-off with someone!

ABOUT THE AUTHOR

Ever since she learnt to hold a pen, Laura Sieveking has loved creating stories. She remembers hiding in her room as a six-year-old, writing a series of books about an unlikely friendship between a princess and a bear.

As an adult, Laura has spent the vast majority of her career working in publishing as an editor. After several years, she decided to put down her red pen and open up her laptop to create a series of her own.

The Academy series is a combination of Laura's favourite things – writing, friendship and sport, all of which take her back to her happy childhood memories of gymnastics training and competitions.

Laura lives in Sydney with her husband and two children.

ACKNOWLEDGEMENTS

A very special thank you to Natasha Ramsden for your expert advice in the creation of this story. And thank you to Rory Brown for sharing your own triumphs and challenges in following the black line.

READ ALL THE BOOKS IN

The Academy of Sport for Girls series.

GYMNASTICS

Can rising gymnastics star Abby make her dreams a reality at the Academy?

Being accepted into the Academy of Sport for Girls was all Abigail Rogers had ever wished for. But before her feet can touch the ground, the gymnasts are thrown into their first competition of the year to determine who will make up the Academy team for the upcoming State Prelims. The pressure is on! Training harder than ever, and with rivalry growing among the students, Abby begins to doubt if she is, in fact, Academy material.

Can Abby up the level of difficulty in her routine and secure a place in the Academy gymnastics squad? Or will she be persuaded to win with dirty tactics?

FROM THE AUTHOR OF ELLA AT EDEN
GIRLS SPORTS ACADEMY
Gymnastics
Abby's Story
LAURA SIEVEKING

ATHLETICS

Can hurdling champion Josie find a way to improve her grades as well as follow her gold medal dreams at the Academy?

With the Academy of Sport for Girls end-of-year Athletics State Finals fast approaching, golden girl of the track, Josie Ingram, and her teammates are training hard. It seems like nothing can stop them from reaching their dreams. However, when Josie finds out she is falling behind in her schoolwork, her world is turned upside down. If she doesn't improve her grades in the upcoming exams, she won't be allowed to compete at the State Finals! Forced to concentrate on her studies and banned from any track practice sessions, Josie feels like giving up. Everything she has trained for will mean nothing if she can't compete.

Can Josie commit to her schoolwork and hold on to her chances of a podium finish? Or will she accept an easy offer that spells trouble?

FROM THE AUTHOR OF ELLA AT EDEN
GIRLS
SPORTS
ACADEMY
Athletics
Josie's
Story
LAURA SIEVEKING

Read on for an extract from
The Academy of Sport for Girls: Athletics

I gently reached up and swept a wisp of my long, strawberry blonde hair away from my eyes. I inhaled and exhaled in deep, measured breaths as I ran. My feet pounded along the path in the rhythm of a trotting horse. *Clip-clop clip-clop.* I was being careful to keep my pace steady – this wasn't a sprint.

I glanced at the sky as I ran. It was only eight o'clock and the sun was already sparkling high in the sky. Heat was radiating down onto my shoulders in the warm spring air. It would be summer again soon. How could it be summer again? I'll admit, my pale, freckly skin is not a fan of the scorching Australian summer. Even with suncream, it will redden throughout the day and either produce more freckles or a hot burn. Never a tan.

Up ahead, I could see Isabella bobbing along the path. You would never have picked Issy as one of the best runners in the state. She was tiny. She had short blonde hair, cut into a pixie bob. Her limbs were muscly, yet thin. She ran longer distances than I did – she had the fitness and speed for the 400 metres and the 800 metres. A little dynamo package.

I wasn't so good at the longer distances. Nope, I wasn't patient enough for all that pacing and counting breaths. I'm more of a quick-dash kind of a girl – I was the 100-metre sprint as well as the 100-metre hurdle champion in my age division in the state. They called me 'golden girl' because nobody could beat me, and my hair always shone red-gold like the medals I won. I smiled to myself. I didn't want to be arrogant – nobody likes a show-off – but you couldn't deny I was the best at what I did. I am Josephine Ingram, lightning bolt runner!

As I snaked my way along the school path, I took in some of the sights around me. We were doing endurance training today. Usually our training was focused on sprints and our specialties, which in my case was hurdles. But occasionally, we did longer distance running to help with our fitness. We had to run our way through the whole campus and back up to the oval again. In most schools that wouldn't be a very big run. But at the Academy of Sport for Girls, it was a great distance. The Academy was huge – it housed Olympic-quality facilities for the best sporting girls in the country.

I ran down the path past the gigantic aquatic centre and past the boarding houses.

I wasn't a boarder, I lived at home locally, but many of the girls in the school had come from the country or interstate. Those girls lived on campus in what I can only describe as mansions!

Once past the boarding houses, the landscape opened up into a vast grassy space. I was heading towards the equestrian stables now, where acres of grass rolled down to the southern end of the school grounds. The grass felt crunchy and dry beneath my feet, a sure sign that this warm spring was about to give birth to a scorching, hot summer.

I breathed harder as the sheer length of the run started to exhaust me.

'C'mon, slowpoke!' a voice laughed as it rushed past me.

I smiled as Nina ran ahead of me. She was my other best friend at the Academy, along with Issy. We had all hit it off immediately in Term One when we began training together. None of us knew anyone else at the Academy and we instantly became inseparable. Nina is one of the kindest people I've ever met – I've never heard her say a mean word about anyone.

I shook my head gently as I remembered those early days at the Academy. I couldn't believe it was so many months ago. And, here I was, in my final term of my first year. After this term, we'd move up to Year 8 and no longer be the babies of the school. It had been the best year of my life.

By the time I'd circled round the equestrian paddocks and snaked my way back through the school, I was exhausted. I could see my friends bent over, panting and huffing as they gulped down water on the oval's grassy centre.

'That was torture!' I huffed as I finished my run.

'No, it wasn't, Josie, it was awesome,' Issy giggled. 'I want to do it again!'

'It was rather invigorating,' said Nina, catching her breath.

'*Invigorating?*' I laughed. 'I love how you use big words to describe everything, Neens.' Not only was Nina a champion runner, she was one of the smartest girls in the whole year. She was a maths whiz and also a genius in English. A lot of our classes were streamed at the Academy, which meant I wasn't in any school classes with Nina. Let's just say, schoolwork wasn't my strongest talent. But I didn't care. You don't need 100 per cent in English to run in the Olympics, do you?

'Girls, start your warm-down!' Coach Jack yelled.

Issy, Nina and I sat on the ground and began to stretch out our legs, still panting.

'Do you reckon we'll get our Maths assessment back today?' Nina asked.

'You wish!' I teased.

'I hope I did okay. Mum said I can't watch TV for the whole weekend if I don't pass,' Issy said, chewing gently on her lip.

'You're lucky to get TV at all!' Nina said.

'My mum only lets us watch it in the school holidays!'

'Ugh, mums can be the worst,' Issy scoffed.

My face reddened and my chest began to tighten a little. I could feel the heat in my cheeks and I quickly looked around for a distraction from the conversation. Issy's eyes met mine. I could see them fill with panic.

'Oh, I mean ... I didn't mean ... I'm sorry, Josie,' she whispered.

'It's all right,' I said, waving my hand casually in the air. 'Dad lets me do pretty much whatever I want! TV anytime, ice-cream for breakfast – he's the coolest.'

Nina and Issy nodded.

'He's pretty awesome, your dad,' Nina smiled.

A bell pierced through the silence.

'That's the warning bell. We'd better go and get changed if we are going to make it to class on time,' Nina said, finishing off her quad stretch.

We bundled ourselves to our feet and took final swigs from our water bottles. I turned back to the oval and gazed at the amazing track and field equipment we had at the school.

'I wish we didn't have to do the school part,' I said wistfully. 'Imagine if we could just do sport, all day.'

'That would get boring,' said Nina.

'And exhausting!' Issy laughed.

I shook my head defiantly. 'No, girls. That would be heaven.'